Apple Tree
Station

Apple Tree
Village

Church

School

Farmyard Tales

The Hungry Donkey

Heather Amery

Adapted by Susanna Davidson

Illustrated by Stephen Cartwright

Reading consultant: Alison Kelly

This story is about
Apple Tree Farm,

Poppy,   Sam,

Mrs.
Boot,

Mrs.
Rose

and Ears,
the donkey.

Ears, the donkey, lived at Apple Tree Farm.

Today, she was
going out.

She was going to
a show.

Mrs. Boot put her in
a little cart.

Poppy and Sam
climbed in.

Off they went.

Mrs. Boot tied Ears to
a fence.

Ears didn't like it. She
pulled at the rope.

Ears was free! She was
also hungry...

"Yum," thought Ears.
"Flowers and fruit."

11

Ears took a big bite.

"Oh no!" cried Mrs. Rose. "My hat!"

Ears ran away.
Everyone chased her.

"Catch that naughty
donkey!" they cried.

At last, Ears stopped.

"I'm so sorry," said
Mrs. Boot.

"Would you like a ride in the donkey cart?"

What fun!

Mrs. Rose rode the cart
in the donkey show.

This time, Ears was
very good. She won
a prize.

Mrs. Rose won a prize too. It was a hat.

It was time to go. "That was fun," said Poppy.

"Mrs. Rose has a new hat. And Ears has a new hat too."

PUZZLES

Puzzle 1

Put these pictures in the right order to tell the story.

A.

B.

C.

D.

E.

23

Puzzle 2

Who's who? Match the names to the people or animals in this story.

Sam

Poppy

Mrs. Boot

Mrs. Rose

Ears

Puzzle 3

Can you spot five differences
between these two pictures?

Puzzle 4

Choose the right sentence for each picture.

A.

Mrs. Boot tied Ears to a fence.
Mrs. Boot tied Ears to a tree.

B.

Ears took a big biscuit.
Ears took a big bite.

C.

Everyone chose her.
Everyone chased her.

D.

"Naughty donkey," said Sam.
"Good donkey," said Sam.

Answers to puzzles
Puzzle 1

1D.

2E.

3A.

4B.

5C.

Puzzle 2

Mrs. Rose

Ears

Poppy

Mrs. Boot

Sam

Puzzle 3

Puzzle 4

A. Mrs. Boot tied Ears to a fence.

B. Ears took a big bite.

C. Everyone chased her.

D. "Naughty donkey," said Sam.

Designed by Laura Nelson
Series editor: Lesley Sims
Series designer: Russell Punter
Digital manipulation by John Russell

This edition first published in 2016 by Usborne Publishing Ltd.,
Usborne House, 83-85 Saffron Hill, London EC1N 8RT, England.
www.usborne.com Copyright © 2016, 1990 Usborne Publishing Ltd.

USBORNE FIRST READING
Level Two

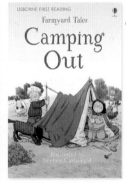